THE PANGOLIN REVELATION

by Lori Schildwachter
illustrated by Laurie Allen Klein

Loran sat in science class learning about animals, his favorite subject. He was learning that all animals have adaptations, body parts and behaviors, to help them survive in their environments.

The teacher gave the class an assignment. Each student would choose his or her favorite animal or invent their own imaginary animal. They had to identify the animal's adaptations and how it used them to survive in their environment. Then the students would create a presentation about their animal to share with the class.

This was Loran's dream assignment! He loved to read and think about animals. He particularly enjoyed drawing them. Loran decided he would mash up all kinds of adaptations to invent a crazy, mixed-up animal like no one had ever seen before.

After school, Loran went straight to his room, sat down at his desk, and began to sketch.

Loran started with a shape. It was a rounded, half circle. It reminded him of an armadillo.

Like most armadillos, his animal would be able to curl up into a ball to protect itself.

"This is a good start," thought Loran. Next, he had to figure out what would cover the animal's skin. Should it have fur, a shell, or feathers? Loran wanted something bolder—like armor. He immediately thought of the scales on a fish. Or even better, a dragon. "Why not both," he said excitedly.

He drew large, overlapping scales just like those found on the Asian dragon fish. These would protect his creature from any predator.

What should this animal eat? Loran thought as he looked around his room for inspiration. On the shelf, he noticed the toy anteater he had gotten at the zoo. That's it! His animal would have a long, sticky tongue to slurp up ants and termites.

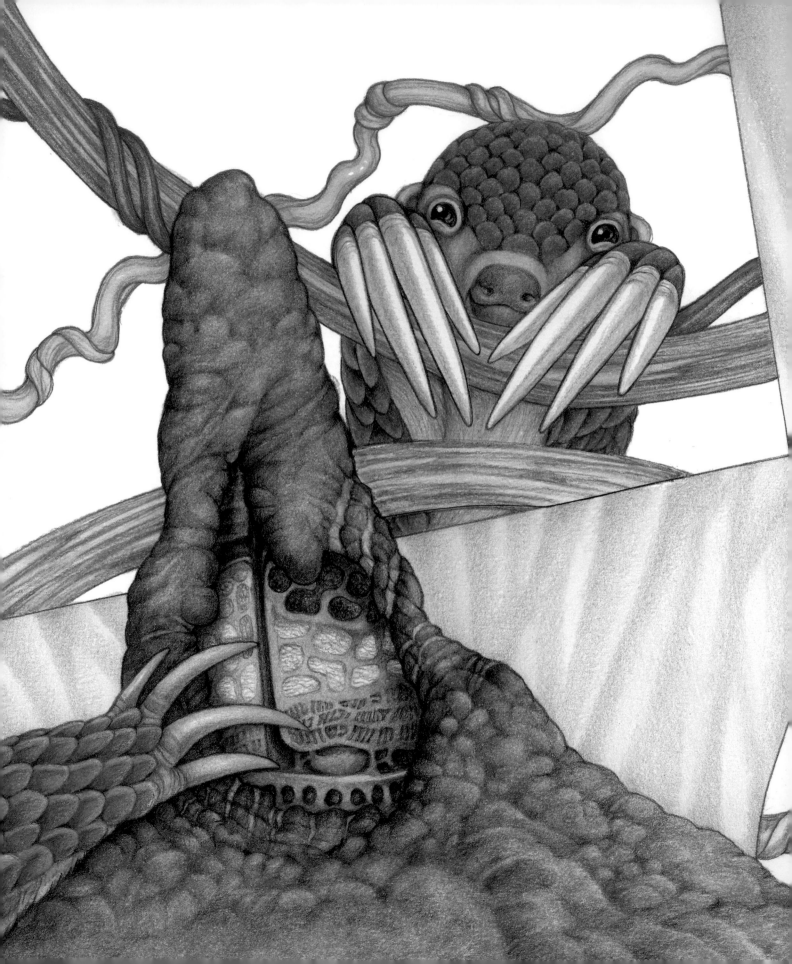

"I will give it some big, strong claws," thought Loran. He began to draw long, thick front claws like a sloth's.

"Hey!" Loran realized, "these giant claws can also be used to dig deep burrows underground for my animal to hide and sleep, just like a gopher tortoise does."

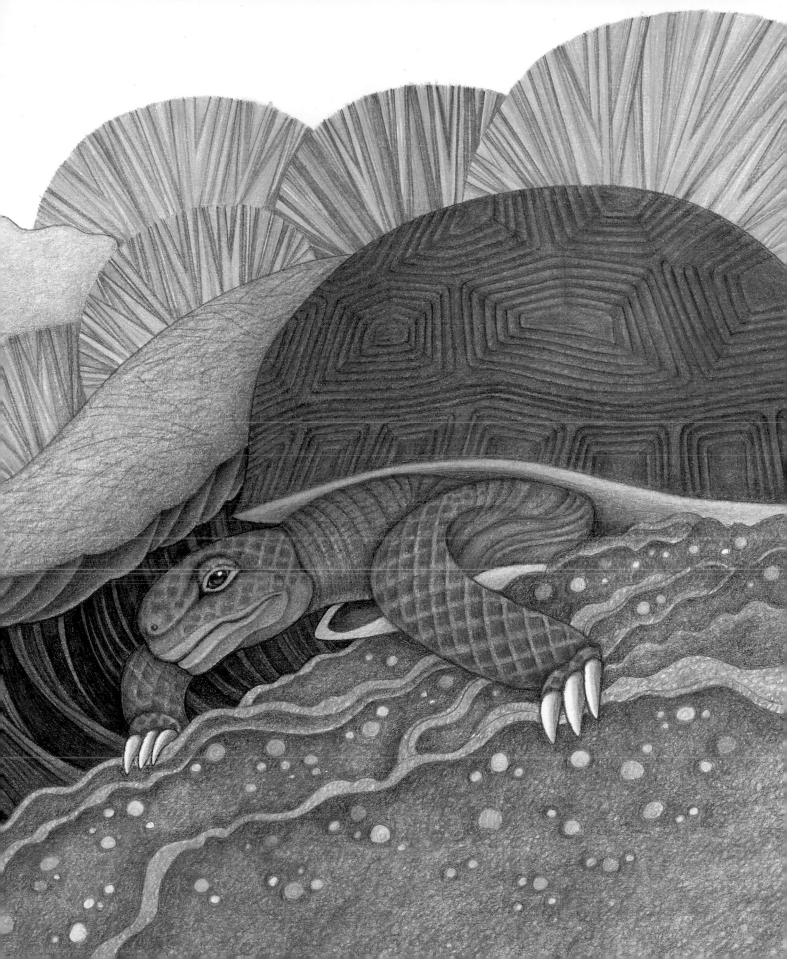

Then it occurred to Loran that the long claws might make it hard for the animal to walk, but he had an idea. "Gorillas can curl their fingers under to walk on their knuckles. That's what my animal will do."

And for added measure, he also decided to give the animal the ability to stand on its hind legs like a bear when it wanted to survey its surroundings.

Things were really starting to click. "I think my animal should also be able to climb trees like a squirrel. This would be another way it could protect itself," he thought.

If the animal can climb trees, it should also have a tail that could hold on to the branches, like some monkeys. Loran added a long tail that could curl around a tree limb.

Loran was very pleased with his animal but decided to add one more final touch. It was a behavior he had seen swans do with their cygnets. This animal would carry its baby around on its back. He drew a cute little baby that looked just like the mom.

There, the animal was done!

Loran sat back and looked at all his notes and sketches. He had taken inspiration for his animal's adaptations from all kinds of species found all over the world and in lots of different environments. It had characteristics and behaviors from mammals, reptiles, fish, and birds all combined into a completely unique animal creation.

"But hold on a minute!" Loran exclaimed, sitting straight up in his chair. He remembered seeing a zoologist on a local TV program a couple of years ago who had brought a strange-looking animal to the set. Loran realized that animal looked just like the creature he had just drawn.

It wasn't an imaginary animal at all, but a REAL one that actually existed! It was a pangolin!

Even more pleased with the way his assignment turned out, Loran carefully signed his name at the bottom of the poster and read the title of his project aloud.

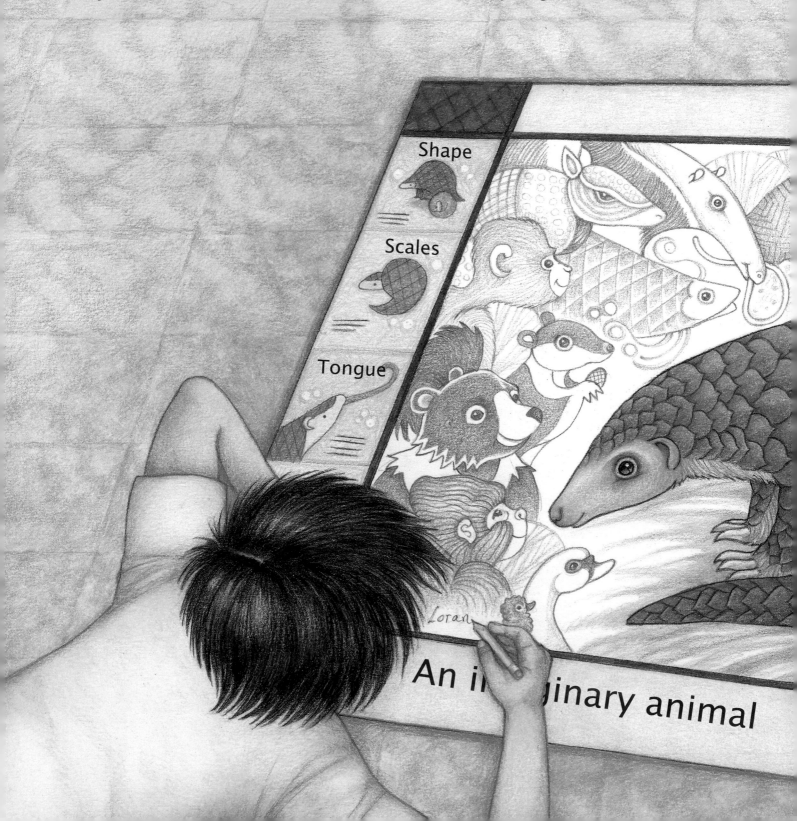

MEET THE PANGOLIN

Climb trees

Prehensile Tail

Walk on knuckles

Stand on hind legs

Carry babies

that really exists

For Creative Minds

What is a Pangolin?

Once more commonly known as the scaly anteater, pangolins have been described as a cross between a dragon, an artichoke, a pinecone, a tiny dinosaur, and an armadillo. The name pangolin comes from the Malay word "pengguling" meaning "something that rolls up." Four species of pangolin are found in Asia, and four are found in Africa.

Depending on the species, they inhabit forest and savannah environments.

Sadly, all pangolins are endangered. Pangolins are relentlessly hunted across all their ranges for their meat and the adaptation that sets pangolins apart from all other mammal species, scales. Thousands of pangolins are killed each year, and some species are facing extinction if effective measures to protect them are not taken soon.

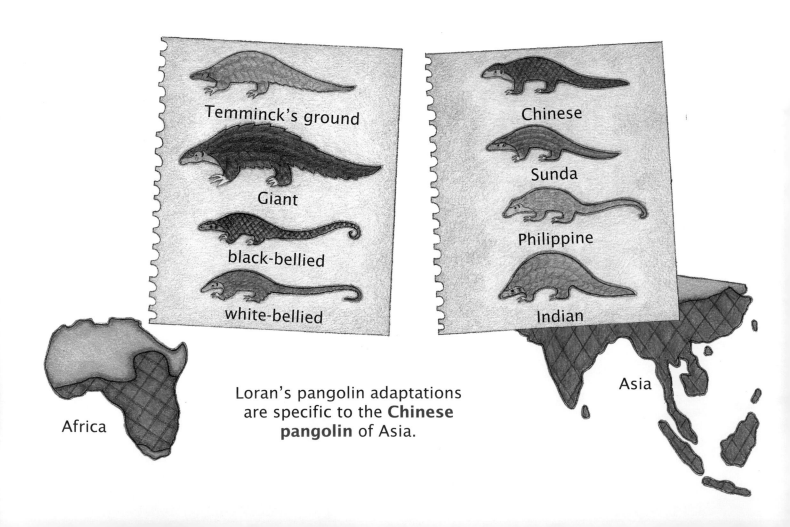

Temminck's ground

Giant

black-bellied

white-bellied

Chinese

Sunda

Philippine

Indian

Africa

Asia

Loran's pangolin adaptations are specific to the **Chinese pangolin** of Asia.

Design Your Own Animal!

Just like Loran designed what he thought would be his own animal, you can too!

Pick an animal shape. Will it be long or short? Flat or round?

What kind of skin covering will your animal have: fur (hair), feathers, or scales? Will it have bones inside or outside (exoskeleton)?

What will the animal eat: plants, other animals, or both? And what kind?

How will it get and eat its food?

Describe the home or shelter your animal uses. Does it make the home or borrow it from another animal? Does it always live in the shelter or just when it has young?

How will your animal move: will it walk (on 2 or 4 feet), fly, or swim?

Describe the habitat where your animal lives. What special body parts or behaviors does it have that helps it live in that habitat?

Will your animal raise its young? If so, how will it carry and care for the young?

Pangolin Adaptations

All living things have body parts or physical adaptations that help them survive in their habitat. Animals also have things they do or behaviors that help them survive. Can you identify whether the adaptations are physical or behavioral?

All pangolins excavate **burrows**, with some species digging very large chambers many feet underground. The burrows are used for sleeping, giving birth, and, in the case of the Chinese pangolin, maybe even hibernating.

Pangolins have 5 toes on each paw. The three curved **claws** on the front paws give them extreme digging ability to tear into termite mounds, excavate burrows, and provide stability for the tree-climbing species.

Some pangolins **climb** trees and sleep in hollow trunks, other species stay on land.

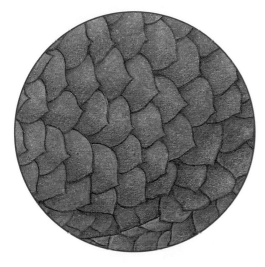

All eight pangolin species have protective **scales** made of keratin, the same material as fingernails and hair.

Pangolins **curl** up into a ball to protect themselves. The ball is so tight that it can't be opened!

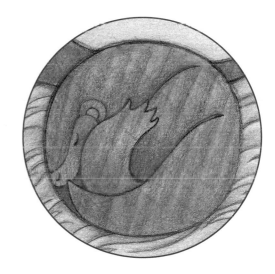

Pangolins **carry** their babies on their backs.

Answers:
Physical: claws, scales,
Behavioral: burrows, climbing, curl into ball, carry babies on their back

This book is dedicated to the memory of Loran Wlodarski, a wildlife appreciator and a dedicated fact-finder. His talents for gathering and sharing information are legendary and he is greatly missed.—LS & LAK

Photo credit for the pangolin on this page is to Adobe Stock Photos (yes, they are real!).

Thanks to Patty Rice, Early Childhood Specialist at the Sedgwick County Zoo and to Jacque Williamson, Curator of Education and Conservation at the Brandywine Zoo, for verifying the accuracy of the information in this book.

Library of Congress Cataloging-in-Publication Data

Names: Schildwachter, Lori, 1962- author. | Klein, Laurie Allen, illustrator.
Title: The pangolin revelation / by Lori Schildwachter ; illustrated by Laurie Allen Klein.
Description: Mt. Pleasant, SC : Arbordale Publishing, LLC, [2021] | Includes bibliographical references.
Identifiers: LCCN 2021013703 (print) | LCCN 2021013704 (ebook) | ISBN 9781643519791 (paperback) | ISBN 9781638170174 (adobe pdf) | ISBN 9781638170365 (epub) | ISBN 9781643519982 (interactive, dual-language, read-aloud ebook)
Subjects: LCSH: Pangolins--Juvenile literature.
Classification: LCC QL737.P5 S35 2021 (print) | LCC QL737.P5 (ebook) | DDC 599.3/1--dc23
LC record available at https://lccn.loc.gov/2021013703
LC ebook record available at https://lccn.loc.gov/2021013704

Bibliography

Pangolin Conservation – Conservation, Education, & Research. pangolinconservation.org. Accessed June 2020.
"Pangolin | Species | WWF." World Wildlife Fund, 2000, www.worldwildlife.org. Accessed Feb 2021
"Pangolin Specialist Group." Pangolin Specialist Group, www.pangolinsg.org. Accessed June,2020.
"Save Pangolins." Save Pangolins, savepangolins.org. Accessed June 2020.

Pangolin Protectors Unite

Do you want to be a Pangolin Protector? Then join others to spread the word about pangolins. Research and support pangolin conservation programs like:

- IUCN SSC PANGOLIN (www.pangolins.org)

- Global Conservation Force (www.globalconservationforce.org)

- Save Pangolins.org (www.savepangolins.org).

Lexile Level: 800L

Printed in the US
This product conforms to CPSIA 2008
First Printing

Arbordale Publishing, LLC
Mt. Pleasant, SC 29464
www.ArbordalePublishing.com